Minis

Ministry of Excuses

by C. Cretagent

Excuse making, down to a Fine Art.

Email: ccretag@hotmail.co.uk

MIE

Ministry of Excuses

CONTENTS
Chapter 0 - Prologue
Chapter 1 - The End
Chapter 2 - Restart
Chapter 3 - Time
Chapter 4 - Cunning
Chapter 5 - Together
Chapter 6 - Album
Chapter 7 - Theft
Chapter 8 - Fishy
Chapter 9 - Gallery
Chapter 10 - Deal
Chapter 11 - Forgery
Chapter 12 - The Club
Chapter 13 - Elections
Chapter 14 - Reward

Ministry of Excuses

MIE

CHAPTER 0

PROLOGUE

An apprentice landed a job working for the secret problem solving agency, the Ministry of Excuses. MIE, for short, was rumoured to be a branch of the British Security Services. Similar to MI5 and MI6, it's inner workings were not widely discussed. In fact, it was so secret that even those who worked at MIE were not even certain it existed!

Operating from a small room in a dilapidated building in South London, the eccentric old man in charge was known as the Professor. Every day was a strange and curious mix of adventure and intrigue.

Ministry of Excuses

MIE Agency shared the second floor of the premises with the erratic French teacher, Madame Dunne. Proprietor of a small French Language School, Madame Dunne and the Professor did not get along well. They only crossed paths when using the shared facilities on the office floor. Mme Dunne would usually be found smoking in the kitchen area and hurl insults at the Professor as he walked past.

However, despite their animosity, Mme Dunne was often the inspiration the Professor's most effective excuses!

It was not widely known that MIE agency was based in that old building. Clients arrived by word-of-mouth directions alone. The legacy persisted, that despite utilising unconventional methods, the Professor had an undeniable knack for getting people out of trouble. Over the years, the Professor had saved the reputations of a number of high profile, unscrupulous figures, by concocting the most amazing excuses. His grateful clients included Company Directors, Accountants, Celebrities, and Member of Parliament, Alan Green.

The Agency's endeavours had previously been scrutinised by newspaper reporter Caroline Wells. She had come close to exposing the Ministry's dirty tricks, and was still hot on their trail.

CHAPTER 1

THE END

By the end of my first week working at the Ministry of Excuses, I was terribly disillusioned. Despite everyday being an adventure, it felt ethically wrong to be using intellect and talent to help fraudulent and dishonest people escape justice.

I looked at the Professor with bewilderment and asked, "Is all you do invent stories to help crooked people wriggle out of trouble?"

The Professor looked hurt and with a wounded expression said, "It's a cruel world out there, and sometimes a few white lies are necessary. You are welcome to leave right now if you are not able to handle that? I can give you your pay and you are free to go?"

I said, "Goodbye then," and he handed me a brown Manila envelope.

"When it comes to work, change is inevitable, except from the vending machine!" Prof said comically. He really didn't seem to care about my departure.

I opened the envelope while walking out the door, and in doing so bumped into Madame Dunne, principal of the French Language School at the end of the corridor.

After a brief chat it was evident that she was not on the best of terms with the Professor. Mme Dunne said I had certainly done the right thing by leaving, and even doubted the validity of the Prof's qualifications.

"He is probably one of those jokers who say they graduated from the so called University-of-Life!" she mocked.

Ministry of Excuses

So, I was not surprised to see there was no money in the envelope. Inside was just a betting slip receipt, for a *Five Pounds* wager on a horse. The slip had odds of thirty to one, for a midday race!

It was already past lunchtime so I went into the betting shop in Clapham Common, where the bet had been placed. To my surprise the horse had won just minutes earlier! I gleefully collected my large winnings, and enquired what time the bet had been placed.

"At 9 a.m. this morning sir," the assistant replied, "the date and time is stamped on the slip," he said, pointing to a line of computerised numbers.

I wondered how did the Professor predict that winner, was it just luck? There were too many coincidences. Yet again, something influenced me to return to the MIE Agency.

CHAPTER 2

RESTART

The Professor was not surprised to see me arrive back the next morning. He was moaning about 'Puff', referencing the French teacher Madame Dunne. The nickname Puff had stuck because she had the personality of a dragon and was a chain smoker! Often to be found in the corridor puffing on a high tar cigarette. Puff had demanded Prof pay half the money to have the stairs and landing redecorated, because it was in the legal agreements to share those costs. However the Professor maintained it was only because of her constant smoking that the nicotine stained walls needed repainting so regularly.

Mme Dunne was pacing up and down outside, with a decorating estimate in one hand and a cigarette in the other. She was muttering in French, and then shouted in English that the Prof was a selfish man with intolerable behaviour. It was the first moment I had sympathy for his situation.

"What subject are you a Professor of?" I asked him.

"Everything, but today my speciality is Physics," he replied, then joked, "just been feeding the cat some nuclear waste ... it now has nine half-lives!"

I forced a momentary smile, but continued with a serious face to ask what the day's agenda was.

Prof explained that business for the agency had been better than ever. So many people were approaching for help, since he had managed to come up with beautiful solutions to a wide variety of problems.

Word was getting around of his skill in rescuing people from the most hopeless situations.

"Problem is," said Prof scratching his head, "we have some rather tricky Government work coming in. A Member of Parliament, Alan Green, is in all sorts of bother; Implicated in a huge scandal and the newspaper reporters are swarming. He wants an excuse to avoid the awful publicity that will ensue, now the newspapers have found out that he has been involved in illegal and corrupt activities."

I listened intently as Prof described the story so far of Minister Green's alleged history of accepting bribes, sabotaging Government records, selling national secrets, and profiting from deals in surplus army weapons. Prof said that Alan Green had become embroiled in this mess because he was being blackmailed to pay off debts he had accrued through casino gambling. Alan had assured him that he wanted to put things right, but the newspapers had already gathered too much hard evidence of his dealings and would not let go of the story.

Wanting to help I had an urge to say, 'Leave this to me, I will solve this problem,' but thankfully managed to hold back those words, because what I really felt like saying was, 'rather you than me!'

The Prof said that he had originally promised to help Alan, but had since changed his mind, as was beginning to believe the case was a hopeless cause. The Professor had concluded that even his genius would be outstretched by this task, and had instead made plans to disappear for a few days and visit his brother who lived on the South coast in Brighton.

"Look after the office while I'm gone, and think of something to say when the MP phones," said Prof as he dragged his brown suitcase, sliding on its two squeaky caster wheels, out the door.

"Just leave this all to me!" I said, kicking myself shortly after!

Now alone, I surveyed the office for inspiration. There was a large brown desk in the middle of the room, a white angle-lamp that could be twisted into all sorts of odd positions and an out-dated computer.

Scattered in the top draw of the desk were piles of betting slips. On closer inspection it seemed that the Professor had put a dozen bets on various horses that other morning at 9 o'clock. So that was how he gave me a winning slip! I realised he had bet on every outcome, and had probably searched the result on the Internet before giving me the winner.

Interestingly there were also seven more betting slips for yesterday's Manchester United versus Liverpool game. All separate bets, covering most combination of likely results. Only the *one all* draw was missing, which was the actual result.

Ministry of Excuses

Clearly he was trying this ruse on somebody else, but who?

There were also various letters from the 'Institute of High Energy Physics' addressed to The Professor, Senior Nuclear Physicist! I started to wonder again what was going on, as it appeared the Prof was now masquerading as a top expert in Radioactivity! This was strange and disturbing.

He had little knowledge of Physics, if asked 'What is a Transistor?' he would probably reply, 'A nun with a sex change!'

As my old science teacher once said, 'Those who falsely pretend to be Physicists, should be sent straight to Prism!'

In the room there was a bookcase and a large dark wooden shelf. Sitting on the shelf was an old 1980's cassette tape player that spent its whole existence playing just one album. The Professor only had one tape, Queen's Greatest Hits, and it had been played thousands of times. The cassette had been worn, chewed and mangled by the tape machine over the years. Each time the player had assaulted his treasured music, the Professor had carefully spun a pencil through one of the reels, and wound the creased extruded tape back into the cassette. There was one section in the song 'We are the Champions' that had been irreparably damaged. The tape at the word *Champions* was so mangled, each time the player came to that section, the music would slur and virtually grind to a halt. The aged motor would try to force its way past the sticking point of the crumpled tape and slur, 'We are the champiooonnnsss' before regaining full speed again for, 'of the world!'

I had suggested earlier that week that the tape was rubbish and should be thrown away. Prof said 'No', explaining in his experience that if you throw anything away which appears useless, it is

Ministry of Excuses

guaranteed that soon after that exact item will be needed for a vital use! I could not see how that old tape could ever be of any use to anyone! I decided to test out the theory, if I threw it away, would it really become useful? Going over to the cassette player, I pressed the eject button, removed the tape and placed it at the bottom of the empty waste paper basket.

The phone rang, I half expected it to be someone asking for a damaged copy of a Queen album, but it was Alan Green MP.

"Alan here, I need some urgent advice," the MP said hurriedly.

"I am the Professor's assistant. How may I help you?"

The MP gasped with relief, "The reporters from the Daily Herald newspaper are on my doorstep. That infuriating Caroline Wells is among them, the political news columnist who is always on my back. She won't go until I give a statement. What shall I say?"

"Tell them that you are taking action for the Good of the Nation!" I advised not really knowing where I plucked that from.

"Great idea, you're the expert so I'll say whatever you tell me. I think I can see where you are going with this," said Alan.

"You do?" I said hopefully, then regained composure and agreed with an emphatic "Exactly."

On the spur of the moment I formulated a plan of action and said, "After you have made your statement to the press, I want you to leave your house immediately and take your family on a mountain climbing holiday in ... Snowdonia!". Although these thoughts were off the top of my head, I reckoned that at least if he was out of the way it would stall for time.

"O.K. Good thinking, I guess the press won't follow me up a mountain!" said Alan with the assured confidence that he was now out of trouble.

"Just stay there for a week, leave things to me, and when you return you will be a national hero." I bragged, sounding more like the delusional Professor every second. Alan was delighted, he had only wanted to get out of the deep predicament he was in, but becoming a national hero would be a real bonus!

Later on that evening the late editions of the London Paper ran with the headline

'MP in Welsh Mystery!'

Alan had followed my advice and told the press reporters that although his recent actions may have seemed unusual, everything he had done was ultimately for the benefit of the Country. He was temporarily retreating to Wales until this had been recognised! The Press commentators wrote that they were completely confused, but the MP had said everything would be explained when he returned from the Welsh Mountains the following week.

When Alan and family had had driven off in their four wheel drive Jeep, they were initially pursued by photographers on motorbikes. However these Paparazzi had tailed off eventually.

By that evening the Green family settled in a remote bed and breakfast hotel, in the heart of Wales, grateful for their break from the limelight.

CHAPTER 3

TIME

The phone rang for the second time that day. It was someone very important, a Doctor Adams from Cambridge University. I had never spoken to a real academic before and was apprehensive as I fielded this call.

"Hello," I stuttered.

"Ah hello, you must be one of the brilliant research graduates that the Professor has told me about?" said Dr Adams.

"Yes, that's right, the Professor has told me all about you," I lied.

"The Professor really is my last hope.

Here at the University I have squandered substantial research grant funding on investigating how to warp time. I published a fake preliminary paper stating we had discovered ground-breaking electo-magnetic principles which could dilate space-time. Further postulating the design of a device similar to a time-machine! Sadly the truth is that we have absolutely no results from any experiments. I am in deep trouble, the University will be furious if they find I have wasted all their money, with nothing to show for it. My career was on the line until the Professor said that your team had actually built a machine that could momentarily warp time. Thankfully he said he will sell the invention to me for a few thousand pounds!"

I could not believe my ears, and shuddered to think what lies the Prof had been spinning.

Dr Adams continued, "I am amazed at

Ministry of Excuses

all the football predictions that your machine can make, this morning I received the betting slip from the Manchester United match, and I checked with the bookmakers who confirmed that bet was placed before the game."

It was now clear why Prof had been putting multiple bets on different outcomes for that match. Again he had covered all the most likely results so he could produce a winning slip!

"Yes, it is an incredible invention!" I said enthusiastically. "We have now produced a bigger machine that can time-warp objects larger than just slips of paper. It is about the size of a microwave oven so I could even put this phone in the time shifting device now if you would like to hear the results?"

"Yes please, a demonstration would be fantastic."

"If I warp this telephone receiver, by setting the rate at which time passes within the machine at say double our earth rate, then all the noises coming from outside the machine will sound as if they are going at the wrong speed. I will turn the radio on to create some background noise."

I switched the Sony machine on to the radio setting and turned it on to full volume.

"Can you hear the radio? I am just about to place the telephone receiver inside our new machine," I shouted.

"Yes, I'm ready," said Dr Adams, who could hear the radio broadcaster finish reading the 12 o'clock news. I looked down to the waste paper basket to retrieve the Queen's Greatest Hits cassette. Just as the Radio presenter was about to play a song, I jammed in the cassette and pressed play. Seamlessly the news ended and the bars of the musical introduction to *We are the Champions*, boomed through the speakers as the tape started turning.

"Powering up the electro-magnetic

Ministry of Excuses

field," I cried. Just as the cassette player reached the damaged piece of tape I shouted, "Warping now."

'We are the champ-ion-sss,' ground deeply out of the machine at half speed, before it sped up again to sing out, 'of the world!'

I turned the player off and pretended to lift the receiver out of an imaginary box and said, "We can only warp time for a second or so, as it requires a huge electromagnetic field, but it's a start."

"It is amazing! Fantastic! Unbelievable! A Miracle!" Dr Adams cried hysterically. "This is the biggest discovery ever known to mankind. Please bring that machine to show me straight away. I will call a press conference to announce this scientific breakthrough, and my job will be saved. I may even be awarded the Professorship I have always dreamed of!"

"Fine. I will bring it on Friday but I must ask you to do something?"

MIE

"Anything," replied Dr Adams, "Anything to see that fabulous machine."

"Make as many inquiries as you can into buying land in Wales. You don't need to actually purchase any land, just act as if want to buy as many square miles of Welsh countryside as possible, preferably near some mountains," I said as an idea came into my head.

Dr Adams thought this was an extremely puzzling request, but was prepared to go along with anything to see this brilliant machine, and save his career.

Alan Green was not the kind of person who could stay out of trouble for very long. He had been walking on the beautiful lower slopes of Snowdonia and enjoying the company of his family for just one day. They had walked in the sunshine, stopping off for refreshments in the small village cafe and taking photographs of breath taking views. For most people this would be an idyllic holiday, his mind was already on other things; in particular how he was going to pay off some of his most recent gambling debts.

Alan had been contacted by a rogue gang of thieves who were planning a raid on an underground bank vault. This secure vault housed a valuable collection of cut diamonds. The criminals had asked the MP to supply them with enough explosives to completely destroy the outer vault doors. The heist plan was to facilitate a rapid break-in by brute force, to steal the precious contents.

Alan had initially said 'No', but the gang had offered him a very tempting share of the takings, and he was beginning to succumb to his inner greed. He pondered on Oscar Wilde's famous quote, 'I can resist everything except temptation!'

Alan thought just one more illegal deal would enable him to sort out his finances.

He said to himself, 'I will use my

contacts in the Ministry of Defence to procure some hand grenades on behalf of the diamond thieves, or should I say diamond wealth re-distributors!'

Later that evening, as his family was finishing their dinner, he explained that he had to go away on urgent government business. He set off in his Jeep to liaise with his crooked army contact, who was able to supply misappropriated military ammunition for the deal.

CHAPTER 4

CUNNING

The Professor was back from his trip and was feeling more optimistic that the Ministry of Excuses could pull off a cunning plan. He spoke to Dr Adams and told him to insist that press conference be held outdoors, in a large remote area away from any public buildings. He explained that this was a necessary safety precaution as the time-machine had not been tested outside of their laboratory before.

Dr Adams was so grateful and remarked, "It is so reassuring that you think of all these things. It is a nice change to work with real professional physicists!"

We went to hire a large white Transit van to transport our fictitious time-bending machine to the press conference. The van would look suspicious if empty, so the Professor filled it with any rubbish electrical junk he could find. An old microwave, radio spares, parts of a bike, as many magnets, coils and any pieces of wire that he could lay his hands on. The Professor then called Alan Green on his mobile phone, and told him to come to the office and pick me up on the way to Cambridge. Alan agreed reluctantly, he did not like the idea of travelling any further than necessary as he had just picked up a consignment of explosives. A crate of hand-grenades were currently sitting dangerously on the back seat of the Jeep.

I was not impressed with the grumpy Alan Green and his lack of manners. Throughout the car journey he was abrupt and impolite, so I decided to raise some of my concerns.

"With all due respect," I said, "why do you deserve any help from us?"

"Oh, trying to bump up your fees now are you? Do you want more money?" sneered Alan.

"Not at all, there is more to life than money."

"What do you want then?" asked the surprised MP.

"Well, it is fair to say that you have not always acted honestly in the past. It would be nice to have an assurance that you intend to mend your ways in the future."

Alan had an indignant expression and retorted, "What I have done is not half as bad as what some of the establishment do. I could tell you some shocking stories of illegal activities and betrayals that go on right under the public's noses."

He went on to tell me about some of the scandals that had been hidden over the years. Alan said that he had heard of undercover agents who had skilfully staged accidents to get certain people 'out of the way'. He gave examples of how statistics were altered and records shredded, when influential people had 'something to hide'. He spoke about how News stories were twisted and embellished by journalists and so called 'spin doctors'

I was shocked. Could all this really be happening in the world?

"So, my theory is … if you can't beat them, join them," said Alan.

"You must not think like that," I pleaded. "This country needs honest people to make sure that justice is done, and good prevails over evil."

"So what do you want me to do about it?"

"I want you to promise that if we solve this problem, you will turn over a new leaf?"

Alan was out of options and reluctantly promised that he would make a new start, and try and do the right thing from now on. Discussing the details of the plan, I said that we would need to stop off somewhere to buy some matches and lighter fuel, to start a small fire to carry off the scam.

"There is no need to stop for matches, I have something on-board already that will start a fire!" Alan said smugly.

CHAPTER 5

TOGETHER

The Professor drove erratically to Cambridge in the lumbering white van, and after what seemed an age, eventually arrived to meet Dr Adams outside the Physics Research Facility. Together they made their way to the unused factory site where he had told the Press to assemble at 3 pm. Dr Adams had arranged for a microphone and two powerfully amplified loudspeakers to be placed in front of a row of plastic chairs.

The Professor parked the large van a short distance behind the microphone stand, and they waited patiently as the press reporters arrived and took their seats.

Caroline Wells from the Daily Herald newspaper was one of the first to arrive. Immaculately dressed in a tweed skirt and jacket suit, a gently contrasting cream blouse, and with her shoulder length blonde hair tied back in a neat bun, this was a reporter who demonstrated attention to detail. This formidable news hound had been tracking Alan Green's actions for months, and amassing a great deal of compelling evidence to expose him.

The tension rose as the reporters and photographers waited for the 3 o'clock announcement. Prof was stalling for time. It was already 3:15 pm and the crowd was getting impatient. Finally Prof stood up to the microphone and started to speak slowly.

"Today, you will see the first demonstration of a most fantastic, awe inspiring, life changing, miraculous, brilliant .."

"Get on with it!" shouted an impatient Caroline Wells.

"... amazing time warping machine!"

The crowd gasped as he continued, "The equipment contained in the back of this vehicle is able to slow the passage of existence around us for a second. I suggest you all look what happens to your watches while we start the demonstration," announced the Professor, as the mobile phone in his pocket started to ring.

It was the French teacher Mme Dunne, chasing up the share of money towards the office redecoration. As Prof answered the phone he held the mobile near the microphone and the whole crowd could hear the conversation.

"Professor, I am phoning about that work, the clock is ticking slowly ..." she said in a menacing French accent.

"I am not sure what work you mean,"

Ministry of Excuses

said the surprised Professor. He then whispered to the crowd, "It is the French Intelligence, they are on to us ... they know we have the time machine!"

"The top level work, our Agents say that you must share it. We will make you pay," Mme Dunne shouted.

The Professor whispered to the reporters, "They are threatening violence and torture."

The crowd was shocked to hear how desperate these people were to get hold of this new invention.

"We will enforce the lease-hold!' Mme Dunne hissed.

"Oh not the lease hold," said the Prof, making gestures of a noose pulled tightly around his neck.

"It won't take long, they can use an industrial gun, it gets results much quicker than the old methods of hundreds of strokes with a thick brush," she cried.

The crowd gasped at the description of

these ruthless methods, but they knew that if International Intelligence were prepared to go to these lengths to obtain this invention, it really must be a fantastic machine!

"Time is money," Mme Dunne screamed, as the Professor gesticulated along with every fitting word she said.

At that moment, Alan's Jeep hurtled round the corner into view.

"Get down. Take shelter. I have explosives!" Alan roared as he jumped out from the Jeep door. He staggered towards the white van clutching a military-grade device. He showed courage and determination as he pulled the pin out of a hand-grenade and threw it under the van, and dived for cover.

There was an almighty explosion, pieces of electrical equipment flew into the sky, and the air shook. Everyone huddled under the plastic chairs as the white van

Ministry of Excuses

burst into flames, its full petrol tank bursting to produce an orange wall of flames.

The fire brigade were on the scene within minutes, hosing down the burning wreck of the van with thousands of gallons of high pressure water, but it was all in vain. All that was left were black smouldering charred remains of the so-called fabulous invention.

After the turmoil had died down, the press conference was continued back at the research laboratory. Dr Adams, Prof, and Alan were huddled in deep and rapid conversation. They stood united, all nodding in agreement with everything being said. Dr Adams shook the Professor's hand warmly before rising to speak.

"Today has been an historic day thanks to the courage of one of our own MPs," said Dr Adams pointing to Alan.

"The Professor and I had devised a

machine that could warp time. It was a combination of years of research, and tireless hard work. It would have changed the world, but in the wrong hands it could have ruined the world. It is true that Alan Green has wrecked our historic research, in his wisdom, knowing that technological advances do not necessarily make life better. How many times, we wonder, have the inventors of the atomic bomb wished they could have destroyed the equipment that they themselves had invented? Ours was only a small time machine, only able to slow time for a second, limited by the size of its small raw earth magnets. Our next project however, was to build a large-scale time shifter, a machine the size of a sky-scraper. Not only would this device have destroyed the environment, the world would have been at wars to obtain this particular land in North Wales, the ideal area where this device could be activated."

Ministry of Excuses

The crowd were deadly silent as they soaked up every word, so he continued, "Mr Green has risked his own life, fearlessly working undercover, and single-handedly destroying the potentially deadly machine that we now appreciate was not a technical advance – but a technical monster."

The crowd cheered, and photographers snapped pictures of Alan looking like the cat that had got the cream!

Dr Adams also looked pleased. He had almost convinced himself that he truly was the creator of a fantastic invention, and that he was prepared to sacrifice all the glory and recognition for the good of humanity!

Only one person in the room was not impressed. Caroline Wells was more than a shade sceptical, and was stunned that people were taken in with this story. Everyone else in the room was wildly ecstatic, shouting, cheering and clapping.

"Alan Green is our National Hero, and we have him to thank for saving Wales, and adding stability to the whole world," shouted the Professor.

The applause and cheers from the audience continued relentlessly, turning into a standing ovation.

Dr Adams lent over to the Professor and whispered, "Did that machine really work?"

The Professor smiled and turned to me and said, "It all worked perfectly, didn't it!"

CHAPTER 6

ALBUM

Despite business going well and the supposedly high profile of the agency's clients, the headquarters of the Ministry of Excuses was lacklustre. Walking up the stairs I assessed the surroundings. A small tatty office room on the second floor of a dilapidated Victorian building. The door had a messy hand-made cardboard sign with *Agency*, scribbled in faded marker pen.

The agency shared basic facilities with Madame Dunne's language school, on the same floor. There was a tiny kitchen that needed a good clean. The Professor said the unimpressive location and poor signage were all part of MIE's under-cover setup!

On entering the office, I found the Professor was already on the phone with a client, engrossed in deep conversation. From the snippets of conversation I overheard, it seemed the topic of discussion related to a dispute over the purchase of a painting. While still in the middle of the call, Prof shouted over enthusiastically.

"We need to put our art hats on to solve this problem. Can you pass me the bottom box from that cupboard," he yelled, pointing to the place where the old records of the agency were kept.

All MIE's recent files were stored on computer, but the older ones were bundled away in dusty cardboard boxes, piled from floor to ceiling. All of these were from well before my time of assisting the Prof. In fact from the identifications on the notes, they went back decades.

Ministry of Excuses

The bottom box had 1911 scribbled across it. It was squashed and torn, and when I struggled to slide it out from beneath the tottering pile. Inside was just one dusty leather-bound photograph album. This ancient album was intriguing. It contained black and white photographs of the Professor. One picture showed him standing next to a man, dressed in old fashioned clothes, who was holding a medium sized painting.

From the setting it appeared that these pictures were taken in Italy about a century ago. This was extremely puzzling, as although I knew the Professor was not young, how could this be him? The shops in the background did indeed have Italian inscriptions on their boardings, and the decor looked distinctively early twentieth century Mediterranean.

This collection of photographs was inter-mixed with Press cuttings, which, too, had 1911 dates. Although written in a foreign language, it was evident the articles were referring to a theft of a famous painting, the *Mona Lisa*, from the Louvre, the renowned Parisian art gallery.

Inspecting the photographs again, it appeared that the painting the Professor was holding looked remarkably like Leonardo da Vinci's classic! My mind was racing. I considered momentarily if the Professor could have been involved in a plot to take the Mona Lisa? However it seemed obvious that my vivid imagination could not possibly reflect the truth. I did not recall ever hearing that the world's most famous painting had been stolen, and concluded these old photos and clippings must be part of an elaborate hoax.

Handing him the album I asked, "These photos of you in Italy, when were they taken?"

"Oh, must be around a hundred years ago ... Gosh, that makes me feel old!"

"How old are you, then?" I enquired disbelievingly.

"Maybe 150? ... Last time I tried to count the candles on my birthday cake I was driven back by the heat!" Prof laughed.

"So that would make you the world's oldest man then?" I said incredulously.

"No," he replied, "my elder brother is older, of course!"

"Huh? Your brother?" I asked.

"Yes, my identical twin. He was born first, just by a few minutes! Our Irish parents were shocked when the two of us popped out. However they should have expected that, as we were born in Dublin Hospital! .. Doubling Hospital, Ha-ha!" he added, attempting to explain his weak joke.

There were times when I could not tolerate the Professor's baloney any more, and this was one of them. I went out for a walk, with no intention of coming back any time soon.

Walking down the stairs, it occurred to me that if the Prof's brother was an identical twin, that could explain how he pulled off a recent scam. The mechanism of the special non-reversing mirror he demonstrated at a conference, may not have been so mystical after all. It could have been done with plain glass, with his twin brother behind, acting out a rehearsed routine. Perhaps they both made the same movements, at the same time, to their own left and right. Giving the illusion that, unlike in normal mirrors, the 'reflection' was not horizontally reversed!

One thing was sure, this old pair of twin brothers definitely had, what they famously call, *The Luck of the Irish!*

Mme Dunne from the French Language school was outside. In one hand she was holding a copy of the Employment section

Ministry of Excuses

pull-out from the local paper, and in the other her trademark cigarette.

Greeting me with a surprisingly cheerful *Bonjour*, she informed me she had applied for a French lecturing job at the local college. It made me consider whether I should be pursuing some kind of further education myself. Perhaps a college course or even on to University to study for a degree.

Life as an assistant, to the increasingly crazy Professor, did not seem to be getting me anywhere.

CHAPTER 7

THEFT

Curiosity always got the better of me. It was a lovely sunny day. I was walking along a winding path banked by beautiful draping trees. I could have had no cares in the world. However the Professor's earlier astonishing words were niggling away at me.

Taking my mobile phone out from my pocket, I did an internet search on 'theft of the Mona Lisa'. To my utter surprise, it was all true, the famous painting was actually stolen on August 1911! One of the most famous paintings in the world, was taken right off the wall of the *Le Louvre*, the national art museum in Paris. It was such an inconceivable crime, that the Mona Lisa was not even reported missing until the following day.

According to the theory of Inspector Lepine, of the Paris police, the thief hid overnight in the Museum after posing as a visitor the day before. The next day was Monday, maintenance day, and the Louvre was closed to the public. The thief waited for the guard to go out for a morning cigarette break. Then, dressed in a workman's tunic, he left his hiding place and removed the Mona Lisa from the wall. The painting was taken down the nearby service stairs and cut from its bulky frame, which Lepine's detectives later found in a dimly lit corner of the stairwell.

The thief then slipped past the dozing security guard in the outer courtyard and disappeared into the anonymity of the Parisian streets. From there, the trail was lost. Leading up to the theft, everyone had been talking about the glass panes that museum officials at the Louvre had put in front of several of their most important paintings. At the time officials were more worried about vandalism than theft. Crazed patrons had attacked famous works with razor blades and acid, so several of the Museum's more prominent paintings, including the Mona Lisa, were selected to have special glass-covered viewing boxes made for them. The public and the press thought the glass was too reflective. Louis Beroud, a painter, decided to join in the debate. He wanted to highlight the issue by painting a picture of a young French girl fixing her hair in the reflection from the pane of glass that had been put in front of the Mona Lisa.

On Tuesday, August 22nd, 1911, Beroud walked into the Louvre and went to the spot where the Mona Lisa had been on display. There, hung only four iron pegs! Beroud contacted the section head

Ministry of Excuses

of the guards, who thought the painting must be at the photographers. The Louvre had recently built a photo studio, and photographing artworks was still a new and exciting concept. So when the Mona Lisa had first gone, staff assumed it was just being photographed.

When it finally dawned that the painting was not in the studio, everybody panicked. The section chief and other guards did a quick search of the museum and realised the Mona Lisa was missing. About sixty investigators were sent over to the Louvre shortly after noon. They closed the Museum, slowly let out the visitors, and then continued the search.

The Louvre was closed for an entire week to aid the investigation. When the national museum reopened, a line of people came to solemnly stare at the empty space on the wall, where the famous painting had once hung. An anonymous visitor even left a bouquet of flowers!

Unfortunately, there was very little evidence to go on. The most important discovery was found on the first day of the investigation. About an hour after the investigators began searching the Louvre, they found the controversial plate of glass and Mona Lisa's frame lying in a staircase.

The French authorities immediately sealed all the borders. They examined every ship leaving, every train coming in and going out. It was impossible to move anything that faintly resembled a work of art out of the country. What they did not know was that the painting was hidden only a mile from the Louvre.

In the weeks following the theft the authorities employed every possible means to find the elusive Mona Lisa. Huge rewards and appeals for help were posted by the Louvre and many of the newspapers. Though the public was restless and the investigators were

Ministry of Excuses

searching, the Mona Lisa did not re-emerge.

Weeks went by, months went by, and then years went by. As time passed, a conspiracy theory developed that the painting had been accidentally destroyed during cleaning, and the museum was using the idea of a theft as a cover-up. In two years that passed, there was no real word about the destiny of the artwork.

In the winter of 1913, over twenty six months after the Mona Lisa was stolen, a well-known antique dealer, Alfredo Geri was approached. He had innocently placed an advert in several Italian newspapers which stated that he was a buyer of *objets d'art,* of every sort, at good prices.

An Italian man with a moustache appeared at Geri's sales office in Florence. After waiting for other customers to leave, the stranger announced he had the Mona Lisa back in his hotel room. The man called himself Leonardo, but his actual surname was later found to be Peruggia. He politely requested a reward of five hundred thousand lire, and an assurance that the painting never be returned to France. Although Geri was tempted to dismiss the man as a fraud, he was intrigued, and made arrangements to view the painting. Geri agreed to the price and suggested they meet in his hotel room the next day.

Following Peruggia's departure, Geri contacted the police, and the following day, they all arrived at the hotel room where Peruggia proudly showed them an old trunk.

Opening the trunk, he pulled out some underwear, a pair of old shoes, and a shirt. Then he removed a false bottom, and there within lay the Mona Lisa. Geri noticed and recognised the Louvre seal on the back of the painting. This was obviously the real Mona Lisa. The painting was confiscated and Peruggia arrested.

Ministry of Excuses

The public went wild at the news of finding the long lost masterpiece. The painting was displayed throughout Italy, before it was returned to France on 30th December, 1913. In January, 1914, the Mona Lisa was ceremoniously restored to her rightful place in the Louvre.

Peruggia was brought to trial in Florence. When he came to court, his legal team included a man claiming to be a Professor of Psychiatry. The defence argument was remarkably simple; Peruggia was an Italian workman, a carpenter who lived a meagre existence, day to day, from hand to mouth. He resented France having the painting, and pined for it to reside in Italy.

He believed that all the Italian masterpieces in the Louvre must have been stolen by Napoleon and brought to France, which upset him terribly. Although Napoleon had looted many of Italy's national treasures during his occupation, the Mona Lisa had belonged to France since Francois I received it from Leonardo himself.

Peruggia's trial was a colourful spectacle. He jumped up and argued with the Judge, who kept banging the gavel and telling him to be quiet. Egged on by the Professor, he argued with the prosecutors, indulged in emotional outbursts and indignant rage, claiming that the Mona Lisa's beauty had bewitched him. He said that his only thought was to rescue her from France, even though he had demanded an exorbitant monetary fee from Geri for the return of the painting.

He contradicted himself many times during his defence at the trial, but ironically, Peruggia became a hero in Italy for his patriotic, though misguided zeal. Public opinion was entirely on his side. In the courtroom, the public gallery would cheer when he said something, and grumble when the prosecution tried to make a point. While he was in jail he was sent bottles of wine, cakes, and even love letters!

Eventually, in defence, the Professor testified that Peruggia was *Intellectually deficient* and the sympathetic Italian tribunal gave him a reduced sentence of seven months. Since by that time, he had already been in jail for nearly eight months, Peruggia was released a free man!

It was astounding that, despite the undisputed facts, he managed to offer a compelling excuse for his actions. Saying that the painting belonged to Italy and should never have been hanging in a French gallery gained public support. He protested he had not really stolen it, but was just trying to return it to its rightful land!

Accepting this incredible excuse, the Italian court, jury, and public accepted the

MIE

theft as a genuine and honourable one. He walked away from the greatest crime of that decade, as a free man. saying it was all for the love of his Country, and because he was bewitched by the painting's beauty

Using this impassioned excuse, Peruggia emerged from the trial being applauded as a national hero, rather than a crooked thief!

Not for the first time, I went straight back to the office to confront the Professor.

CHAPTER 8

FISHY

"How is this possible?" I asked, showing Prof the article about the Italian jury reaching the not guilty verdict.

"Oh yes, well spotted; that was my idea, and I saved Peruggia's scalp. It was a great excuse. Claiming he was doing it for the country is always a good line," the Professor said with a sly smile.

"No, I mean how possibly could it be you? Really You, in Italy, a century ago?" I demanded pointing at the photograph.

"We've done international work in the past, I've toured many countries in this line of work," the Professor said. "It is not just the U.K. that needs excuses you know."

There was no real explanation coming from Prof to answer my 'How' question. Mysterious as ever, he avoided the subject. Every time I asked about his actual age, he would laugh off my question with jokes such as:

I'm at the age when my back goes out more than I do!

Any questioning was fruitless.

Prof handed me a bag containing a blank white canvas, and a set of artist brushes and oil paints.

"I need you to forge a copy of the Mona Lisa painting," he said.

"I'm no artist," I remarked, "I haven't painted anything since school days."

Prof said it did not matter how accurate my painting was, just a basic image would be enough to lift MP Alan Green out from another spot of bother.

Ministry of Excuses

"I should have guessed it was him on the phone," I murmured.

"Alan is our most regular customer!" the Professor replied.

"Yes, and he is not the smartest of people," I quipped, "if he took an IQ test, it would come back negative!"

I decided to take a visit to the local college, to ask if I could use their art studio facilities to create the painting. It was a place I had been wanting to check out since Mme Dunne had mentioned her new job. Hoping she could be a useful contact, I headed for the French department to see if Mme Dunne could direct me to the right people, and possibly *'pull a few strings.'*

Mme Dunne was in the middle of teaching a class when I arrived. The door was wide open and there was a racket coming from a disruptive group of teenagers. It did not surprise me that there was no classroom control, and it sounded as if Mme Dunne was in terrible mood. It was questionable how such an unstable chain smoker would survive a whole hour without a cigarette anyway!

I could hear the students laughing and making fun. Mme Dunne had walked past every desk collecting coursework from each student. The homework had been to complete a project about the French Revolution. There had been a whole exercise of difficult questions that one student, Bill, had not had the motivation or inclination to complete. He had decided that playing computer games was far more interesting.

Bill had not handed in anything, and Mme Dunne stood in front of the class demanding that he gave an explanation, which did not revolve around his standard 'The dog ate it' excuse.

"The fish ate it!" Bill joked.

The class laughed, and Mme Dunne

Ministry of Excuses

gave a slight smile, which quickly faded.

"Oh, tres drole. Where is your homework Bill?" Mme Dunne growled, with an impatient tone.

"If I said it was lost, would that sound a bit fishy?" Bill teased, as giggles came from the rest of the class.

Mme Dunne exploded, "I want to know why you have not done my set work, and do not dare mention any fish."

"Good COD!" Bill replied to a rapturous roar from the other pupils.

"What kind of PLAICE is this?" he continued.

"Bill, Arret! Maintenant!" Mme Dunne said in a raised voice.

"You think my excuses are just red-HERRINGS!"

"B I L L !" Mme Dunne screamed.

"I put my heart and SOLE into trying to do the homework, but am now getting BATTERED, please let me off the HOOK?" Bill jeered, as the class screamed with delight.

"Get out, now!" Mme Dunne fumed.

"Ta Ta, or should I say TARTARE," Bill whispered as he left the room!

CHAPTER 9

GALLERY

MP Alan Green had recently won a promotion, thanks to the Professor's help turning his previous blunders into successes. He was now Minister for the Environment. Not the top job in the Government, but it was a Cabinet post, from which he could progress even further. In the back of his mind was the fact that the current Prime Minister was due to retire in the summer on health grounds, and there was no lack of ambition in Alan Green's unrelenting desire to hold the highest ranked position as leader of the country.

Alan's only worry was financial. Still on his mind was an outstanding debt which was overdue for payment. Since he had promised to stay out of trouble from now on, he could no longer be involved in any devious deals to obtain the required cash. Alan now regretted having wasted all the money he had previously gained from lucrative bribes. The previous month he had spent over fifty thousand pounds on a painting from the prestigious *Caesar* Art Gallery.

He thought it would be an investment which could make him a good profit, but sadly on this occasion it was he who was the victim. When making the purchase of the watercolour entitled *Le Chateau*, by an upcoming Belgian artist, he was promised that it was worth a small fortune. At the price it was offered for sale, it appeared to be an absolute bargain.

Alan Green only realised that this was an elaborate con, when he phoned the art gallery the next week enquiring what price they would offer to buy the picture back. He was shocked when they offered a figure in the region of one hundred pounds.

"One hundred?" Alan shouted in disbelief.

"I am sorry sir, but prices in this market do fluctuate," replied Mr Pontier, curator of the gallery.

"But I paid fifty thousand for it just weeks ago!" Alan protested.

"If you read your purchase contract small-print, you will see we are under no obligation to repurchase stock at any price," responded Mr Pontier, in a firm tone.

Alan reflected on what a hard time he was having leading an honest life, especially when he was surrounded by businessmen like Mr Pontier, who were more crooked than himself. Now faced with this unsolvable predicament, he did the only thing that could possibly help; he phoned the Prof, requesting an urgent appointment.

Later that day the MP arrived at MIE agency office. He marched in briskly, carrying the *Le Chateau* painting that he had purchased for fifty thousand pounds, under his right arm, and a sheet of paper in his left hand.

"Here is the stupid painting, and the contract of sale," Alan said holding out the sheet of A4 paper.

I had been reading up on the Mona Lisa painting that the Professor wanted copying. It seemed pertinent to research some background information on the artwork before attempting the enormous task of duplicating it.

The web pages stated that historians believe the painting is a portrait of Madam Lisa Giocondo, who lived in Florence, Italy. It is a painting that has been incredibly well preserved, it is smaller than most people expect at just seventy five centimetres tall. Crafted with oils, not on canvas, but on a fine-grained white poplar wood board. Started in 1503, Leonardo worked on the painting for over four years, carrying it with him during his travels and parting with it only at his death.

In a break with the Florentine tradition of outlining the painted image, Leonardo perfected the technique known as *sfumato*, which translated literally from Italian means vanished or evaporated. Creating imperceptible transitions between light and shade, and sometimes between colours, he blended everything without borders, in the manner of smoke, with brush strokes so subtle as to be invisible to the naked eye.

Leonardo was fascinated by the way light falls on curved surfaces. The gauzy veil, Mona Lisa's hair, and the luminescence of her skin, are all created with layers of transparent colour, each only a few molecules thick, making the lady's face appear to glow, and giving the painting an almost magical quality. Even the use of landscape as background was a departure from tradition.

After his death, Leonardo left the portrait to his close friend, Francois I of France. The king hung Leonardo's treasure in a prominent place in the bathroom in the palace at Fontainebleau, where visitors from all over Europe admired her.

It is said that the Louvre art museum was born in the French king's bathroom. He had so many paintings in his private quarters that the area was converted to a semi-public art gallery. When Louis XIV moved the French court to Versailles, he took the Mona Lisa with him. However, his son, Louis XV, hated the picture and ordered it removed from the palace. For a time it wound up in the hands of a palace

Ministry of Excuses

bureaucrat and during the chaos of the French Revolution, it was hidden in a warehouse. When Napoleon came to power, the enigmatic lady was restored to a place of honour in the emperor's luxurious bedroom.

The painting was brought to the Louvre when it first became a public museum just over two centuries ago, and has been there ever since, apart from the two years when it was stolen in 1911.

CHAPTER 10

DEAL

Mme Dunne asked the Director of the college if it was possible to for me use their art room for a special project. They had agreed that it would be fine, out of normal student hours, to attempt the painting with their facilities. Mme Dunne whispered she had not told the college that I was working on a secret assignment, of great national importance.

This took me by surprise, as this was the first time she had ever appeared to take MIE's work with any seriousness. Usually she would ridicule any of the Professors scheming plans.

I asked, "Madame, have you changed your opinion on our agency?"

"Un peu, a little, perhaps," she replied. "I know you and the Professor get results ..."

At this point it was evident that Mme Dunne's unusual helpfulness may be coming at a price.

"I have a petite problem of my own you may be able to assist with?" she continued, while lighting up a cigarette.

"Oui, Oui?" I responded.

She took a long puff on the strong cigarette and sighed, "I have a very problem student, his name is Bill, he interrupts my classes with jokes about Fish. He wont stop. If he likes fish so much, perhaps you can arrange that he has a messy encounter with some?"

I thought back for a moment, and recalled the way Bill disrupted her lesson. His actions were detrimental to the education of the other students. Thinking ethically, with a Utilitarianism viewpoint, it would be for the overall greater good if Bill was discouraged from his Fishy Behaviours. I agreed that when all this was finished, I would talk to Prof.

"Maybe we can catch up with Bill, and arrange that he has a *whale of a time* going on a fish related voyage," I joked.

"Send him on a one way trip to Finland, or Trouter space!" Mme Dunne laughed.

CHAPTER 11

FORGERY

It took most of the weekend to paint a copy of the Mona Lisa. Deep in concentration, nothing would distract me from the masterpiece I was creating. It was fun being an artist, a cheating artist at that. I had traced a small picture of Mona from a book, and enlarged the outline on a photocopier until it was the correct size. Then it was just a task of painting by numbers, filling in the regions with the correct shades of oil paint; but it was not easy. The copy still looked nothing like the original.

The painting was never really finished,

there was just no way to make anything approaching an accurate copy of the real masterpiece. However Prof seemed happy with it, and said it would be quite adequate to carry off his plan to obtain the return of the fifty thousand that Alan had paid for *Le Chateau* painting.

After studying the contract of sale, Prof had discovered that there was only one ground on which the Caesar gallery would ever refund the money expended on any piece of art. Clause twelve said that the gallery would make an exceptional full refund of fees paid if the art piece could be subsequently proved to be a forgery, and not the work of the purported artist.

Prof hatched a plan. He used double sided sticky tape to attach my copy of the Mona Lisa upside down, on to the back of *Le Chateau* painting. With everything in place, the Professor experimented quickly turning the canvas, spinning the dual paintings around their diagonal axis.

Ministry of Excuses

Holding the canvas at opposite corners, one hand on the top right, and the other on the bottom left edge, he could rapidly flip which appeared. One moment the beautiful chateau could be seen, the large stone built castle in its acres of lush grass. The next moment, the fake Mona Lisa was displayed, with her following eyes and enigmatic smile.

Prof agreed to meet Alan outside the Caesar Gallery. In a cloth bag he carried the prepared *Le Chateau* painting, with the forgery taped to the back. They had arranged to meet at 2 p.m. on a day when there was an auction of prestigious works, so they could be sure at that time the gallery would be full of authoritative and well-respected art critics.

When Prof and Alan marched into the premises, a small bell on top of the door tinkled, gaining the attention of the customers in the shop. There were a number of well-known art collectors present, along with various directors of rival galleries, who had come to survey the competition, and monitor the prices that works were fetching at auction. These onlookers watched with interest as the two men walked up to the sales counter to confront the curator of the gallery, Mr Pontier, who had sold them the watercolour painting.

"Excuse me Mr Pontier, I wish to have a full refund on this painting. I have had it examined by Professor What, a distinguished expert in the art world, and he informs me that this painting is a disgraceful forgery," said Mr Green, as the Professor pulled the painting out of the bag, showing him *Le Chateau*.

"You must be mistaken my dear friend," replied Mr Pontier, patronisingly. The Professor turned to the group of people watching nearby, as he did so he flipped the canvas to show my awful copy of the Mona Lisa. The observers made

Ministry of Excuses

disapproving noises, which started as gasps and tuts, then developed into laughter.

"That is the worst forgery I have ever seen," shouted a dignified looking lady.

"Mr Pontier, you have surpassed yourself with this sale, even we did not think you would stoop this low," said another.

"It is a terrible forgery. I have seen the original in Paris," called out an elderly gentleman.

The Professor flipped the painting back to reveal *Le Chateau*, as he turned it towards an extremely embarrassed Mr Pontier.

"I am not sure what could have happened," Mr Pontier gulped, "but I will give you a full refund right away."

The red-faced Mr Pontier hoped that the laughter of the crowd would die down. He issued an immediate refund of all money paid, to save his tattered reputation.

The Professor and Mr Green left the shop celebrating the return of the purchase fee. As they stepped out onto the pavement, the Professor could have sworn that he saw a blonde woman in a long overcoat following behind. Her walk seemed reminiscent of that of the investigative newspaper journalist who had caused so much distress to the Professor in the past.

The conversation about their recent success was far too deep to be interrupted by random distractions, but The Professor allowed himself a quick glance round. The street was empty and there was no one to be seen.

CHAPTER 12

THE CLUB

The Professor had a new client, a top league football club. The Club's Manager, and the Club's top player had both been caught by police violating traffic laws and were facing prosecution, and a certain fine and driving suspension.

On the face of it both cases were inexcusable: the Manager had been caught in his BMW, which was driving along the hard shoulder of the Motorway, this lane being reserved only for emergency breakdowns.

The incident happened when there was traffic jams on all three driving lanes, and the impatient Manager instructed his driver to take the car at high speed down the emergency hard-shoulder. A police vehicle had followed the BMW and pulled over the vehicle, and at the time the Manager could offer no reason for breaking the motoring law. other than being in a hurry to return to the club grounds.

The other case involving a top player, involved a speeding charge, going too fast for the road limit.

The Professor was pacing around the room. He was annoyed as had been waiting to use the shared bathroom facilities that MIE and Madame Dunne both used. She often locked herself in there to smoke a cigarette, or two! The frustration of waiting had given him an idea.

When the football club's lawyer called, he suggested an excuse to use as a defence argument for driving out of lane.

Ministry of Excuses

"The Manager can tell the judge that he was driving in the hard-shoulder due to a biological emergency. He was suffering from campylobacter virus, which causes severe diarrhoea," said the Prof.

"Do you think the Judge will believe that excuse?" the lawyer asked.

"Sure, give some details. Stomach cramps were an immediate warning that if he did not get to the club to use the bathroom as quickly as possible, the consequences would have been unimaginable."

"Worth a try," mused the Lawyer, "and for the player with the speeding charge?"

"He was forced to drive fast, to escape the chasing trail of newspaper reporters. Refer to the pursuing photographers, as the *Paparazzi,* for added effect!"

When the Prof finished the phone call, I confronted him on the ethics of using such tenuous excuses.

"It is often easier to ask for forgiveness,

than permission!" the Professor said.

He continued to explain that in general making excuses is a fine art that requires a delicate touch. It is important to be somewhat factual, but not necessarily too honest. In the cases of football stars, any lame excuse will do. The more implausible an excuse sounds, the more likely the public will think that it must be true. Intuitive logic dictates that nobody would offer a ludicrous reason, unless it really was the case!

The Professor took an ethics text-book from the shelf, and flicked through the pages.

"There are as many different ethical theories as there are chapters in this book," he said in a justifying tone.

He went on to say there various models for what might constitute *Ethical* behaviours, and gave examples which highlight potential paradoxes.

One group might advocate

Ministry of Excuses

Utilitarianism, meaning act in the way that does the most overall good. Another school of thought, Deontology, states obeying the law is paramount, regardless of consequences.

"I am not a Deontologist," said the Professor, "they believe it is wrong to break any rules, but I think there are exceptions."

I conceded every ethical dilemma can have a different best outcome, depending on viewpoint.

I thought for a moment and replied, "Football players can't be ethical deontologists then, as they wont cross any line!"

The court cases went in favour of the football club, and both sports personalities were given the benefit of the doubt. Not-guilty verdicts were returned.

Reporter Caroline Wells had been observing the proceedings in court, and was incredulous. She had heard the phrase 'the law is an ass' but she felt something had to be said.

While the Professor had notched up two more successes to add to the agency's credits, Caroline Wells had added two more reasons to publish a tell-all story!

To this day, referencing the lavatory reason for breaking traffic laws, is known in some legal circles, as the 'Football Manager's defence.'

CHAPTER 13

ELECTIONS

Alan Green was excited to be moving into new offices, just a minutes walk from the debating chamber in the Houses of Parliament. It was a large stately room, with oak veneer lining the walls, and deep red plush carpet that created a sea of luxury. He did not have a top post in the cabinet. Minister for the Environment was not as prestigious position as heading the department of Health, Education, Foreign policy or Defence. Nor did he have many true friends among the ministerial colleagues. Many were sceptical of his previous scrapes that the Professor had managed to excuse him from.

The general public had, on the whole believed every word of it, but there were a number of MPs who had the same poor impression of him as Caroline Wells did.

"You can fool some of the people, some of the time," he mused, "but you can not fool all of the people, all of the time!"

Alan Green did not really care what people thought, and believed it was a case of mind over matter.

"I don't mind, and they don't matter!" he giggled to himself.

Although in reality, at that crucial time, public opinion ratings DID matter greatly to all the cabinet ministers for one very important reason. Elections for the new head of the party were looming, as the Prime Minister was soon retiring following complex heart bypass surgery. Alan was barely in the frame for succeeding a Prime Minister who had been the most popular

Ministry of Excuses

leader for over a century. The forecasters predicted that the contest would be a close run between the current Minister for Education, and the Chancellor of the Exchequer. Alan's chances of moving into number Ten Downing Street were thought to be lower than a hundred to one. Something had to done to increase his standing amongst the other MPs before they would elect him leader.

As Alan sat down at the desk he caught sight of a familiar face at the door.

Recognising the smartly-dressed woman as the reporter Caroline Wells, from the Daily Herald, he started to worry what she was doing there. He knew she was far from being one of his admirers.

"Please come in, how may I help?" Alan said politely.

"You could start by resigning right now," Caroline said throwing a large ring binder on the table. "This dossier is full of evidence documenting your appalling

MIE

behaviour over the last year. Every misdemeanour, bribe, and unacceptable action you have been involved in, is listed in detail in this file!"

"I have never been found guilty of anything," Alan protested.

"Unbelievably no, you are like a cat with nine lives. Your partner in crime, that Professor has inexplicably saved your neck time after time, and all that is documented in the file as well. You two are a pair of despicable charlatans."

"So what do you want?" Alan asked.

"Resignation. You are not fit to be in office, and certainly not responsible enough to be in charge of our environment," said Caroline, glaring forcibly.

"I am not leaving this department, I have only just got this job!" Alan said indignantly.

"If you do not resign, I will publish this damming dossier of facts on the morning

Ministry of Excuses

of the leadership election. It would make very interesting reading. Here is my business card, ring when you have made a decision on which way it is going to be."

As Caroline Wells left the room, Alan Green looked at the business card that contained the email address, and phone number of the newsroom at the Daily Herald. Rather than calling that number, he picked up the phone, and called the MIE Agency.

When the Professor heard what had happened a drained look rushed over his tired old face. The bubble was about to burst, the details of their scams were to become public and there would be serious ramifications.

The Prof paced up and down, trying to think of a solution. He picked up the phone and called Caroline Wells, and she agreed to meet us for lunch.

By talking up Alan Green's virtues, we

tried to persuade Caroline not to bring Alan and his family into disrepute. However she was not deterred.

"These details of MP Green's antics are any reporter's scoop, a story of a lifetime," explained Caroline, "I have been overlooked for promotion this year. Without proper recognition I may be stuck in the same position at the Daily Herald forever."

The Professor could not deny that publishing this scandal would raise Caroline Well's profile in the industry.

"What is the highest position that a newspaper reporter aspires to?" I asked.

Caroline answered, telling us what her ideal top job in the media would be, and it gave the Professor an idea for a plan.

On the morning of the leadership election, Alan came down for breakfast. He dared hardly look at the newspaper. He had not resigned as Caroline had demanded, and he expected to read the worst damming article about him in the Daily Herald.

"Have you seen what they have written about you in the paper?" enquired Mrs Green. Alan's heart sank. He picked up the Daily Herald and read the headline,

'GO GREEN FOR PRIME MINISTER.'

The article was astoundingly full of praise for Alan. The impassioned piece advocated his intelligent, charming, charitable, brilliant and caring personality. It gave convincing arguments on why he really was the only candidate fit to carry on the role of the previous Prime Minister.

Alan could not believe what he was reading, the gallant man that was described in the paper did not sound one bit like himself, in fact it was the complete opposite, but he enjoyed reading it anyway. He read it over and over again, nearly a dozen times.

That afternoon, the corridors of parliament buzzed with electrified excitement as the MPs walked into the great hall to cast their votes. The magnificent parliament chamber, stooped in centuries of tradition, was electrified with nervous chatter as the votes were counted.

The election results were a very close run, but the positive article in the Daily Herald had persuaded many of the undecided ministers to vote for Green at the last minute. He was successfully selected as party leader by a tiny margin, winning a majority by just one vote!

CHAPTER 14

REWARD

Standing on the steps of number Ten Downing Street, Prime Minister Alan Green commenced reading an outstanding acceptance speech. The words had eloquence, sensitivity and common sense, which was intellectually beyond this MPs usual level.

It would be disclosing too much to reveal who penned that masterpiece, but let us just say it was better than the authors artistic skills copying the Mona Lisa!

Alan spoke about leading a Government that would tackle poverty, and fight for equality. Pledges to build a country that would lead with technology, but not forget nature and the environment. The speech continued with commitments to integrity, honesty and justice for all. He finished by thanking those that had helped elect him, and ended with an important announcement.

"I would like to introduce you to the Government's new Press Secretary," he said to the flash of camera lights.

"The talented, brilliant, Caroline Wells."

Printed in Great Britain
by Amazon